Henry VIII
Has to Choose

by Julia Jarman
Illustrated by Gary Northfield

W
FRANKLIN WATTS

About this book

The characters and story are based on real events in history. Henry VIII (1491–1547) was crowned king in 1509 at the age of just 17 and he went on to reign for 38 years. In that time he was very busy – waging wars, learning tennis, robbing monasteries of their gold and building palaces. He also had 6 wives: Catharine of Aragon, Anne Boleyn, Jane Seymour, Anne of Cleves, Kathryn Howard and Katherine Parr. There is a famous rhyme that helps you remember what happened to each wife:

"Divorced, beheaded, died;
Divorced, beheaded, survived."

First published in 2009 by
Franklin Watts
338 Euston Road
London
NW1 3BH

Franklin Watts Australia
Level 17/207 Kent Street
Sydney
NSW 2000

Text © Julia Jarman 2009
Illustrations © Gary Northfield 2009

The right of Julia Jarman to be identified as the author
and Gary Northfield as illustrator of this Work has been asserted
in accordance with the Copyright, Designs and Patents Act, 1988.

A CIP catalogue record for this book is available
from the British Library.

ISBN 978 0 7496 8573 7 (hbk)
ISBN 978 0 7496 8579 9 (pbk)

Series Editor: Melanie Palmer
Series Advisor: Dr Barrie Wade
Series Designer: Peter Scoulding

Printed in China

Franklin Watts is a division of
Hachette Children's Books,
an Hachette UK company
www.hachette.co.uk

King Henry VIII wanted
to get married – again!

He had been married before,
but things hadn't worked out.
He wanted a wife to give him sons.

But his wives kept having baby girls! Catherine, his first wife, had a girl called Mary – so he divorced her.

Henry's second wife, Anne, had a girl called Elizabeth. He went mad with rage and he had Anne's head chopped off!

Jane, his third wife, gave Henry a son but then she died. His son, Edward, was often ill and doctors thought he might die, too.

"I need another wife," Henry told his courtiers. "A young, pretty one who will give me lots of healthy sons."

All the courtiers began to look for a new wife for Henry.

Henry sent Hans Holbein,
the court artist, to find him
a suitable princess.

"Paint me pictures of them all," he ordered Hans. "I will choose the prettiest one."

While he was waiting, Henry had his own portrait painted. But the portrait made Henry very cross.

14

"That looks nothing like me!"
he roared. "I'm not that old!
Or that fat! Or that bald!"

It took the artist a long time
to paint a portrait that pleased
the king.

By the time he had finished,
Hans Holbein had returned
with pictures of the princesses.

Henry liked the portrait of one
princess, called Anne of Cleves.
"She's young and pretty," he said.

"And look at her jewels. She must be rich!" He signed the marriage contract at once.

"Bring Anne to my palace," Henry said to his courtiers. "And take her this portrait of me," he said proudly.

Henry could hardly wait to see his new wife – or for her to see him.

While Henry waited for his new wife, he went out hunting.

He danced ...

and he played tennis.

He also held lots of feasts,
so he got even fatter.

25

Then Anne arrived – and she didn't recognise Henry. "You look nothing like your portrait!" she screamed. "You are old – and very fat!"

"And you're ugly," roared Henry, "I'd rather marry a horse!" But it was too late. The marriage contract had been signed.

But Henry got his way – as usual.
He divorced Anne six months later.

Then he began looking for wife
number five ...

Puzzle 1

Put these pictures in the correct order.

Which scene do you find most important?

Now try writing the story in your own words

Puzzle 2

Word Bank

Dancing
Eating
Feast
Hunting
Portrait
Tennis

What do these pictures tell you about

Henry VIII and the way of life at the time?

How are things different today?

You can use the word bank to help you.

Answers

Puzzle 1

The correct order is: 1d, 2a, 3b, 4f, 5c, 6e.

Puzzle 2

Life was very different during King Henry VIII's lifetime. Think about court, palaces, outdoor activities and food. To find out more, try this book:

Henry VIII, (History Makers), Sarah Ridley, Franklin Watts 2009

Look out for more Hopscotch Histories:

Henry VIII Has to Choose
ISBN 978 0 7496 8573 7*
ISBN 978 0 7496 8579 9

The King and the Great Fire
ISBN 978 0 7496 8575 1*
ISBN 978 0 7496 8581 2

Florence and the Drummer Boy
ISBN 978 0 7496 8574 4*
ISBN 978 0 7496 8580 5

Ben's Escape from the Blitz
ISBN 978 0 7496 8578 2*
ISBN 978 0 7496 8584 3

The Song of Boudica
ISBN 978 0 7496 8576 8*
ISBN 978 0 7496 8582 9

Eric Bloodaxe, the Viking King
ISBN 978 0 7496 8577 5*
ISBN 978 0 7496 8583 6

Toby and the Great Fire of London
ISBN 978 0 7496 7410 6

Hoorah for Mary Seacole
ISBN 978 0 7496 7413 7

Remember Remember the 5th of November
ISBN 978 0 7496 7414 4

Pocahontas the Peacemaker
ISBN 978 0 7496 7080 1*
ISBN 978 0 7496 7411 3

Grandma's Seaside Bloomers
ISBN 978 0 7496 7412 0

Tutankhamun and the Golden Chariot
ISBN 978 0 7496 7084 9*
ISBN 978 0 7496 7415 1

For more Hopscotch books go to: www.franklinwatts.co.uk

*hardback